Katie Woo's

✳ Neighborhood ✳

Helping
Mayor Patty

by Fran Manushkin

illustrated by Laura Zarrin

PICTURE WINDOW BOOKS
a capstone imprint

Katie Woo's Neighborhood is published by Picture Window Books,
a Capstone imprint
1710 Roe Crest Drive
North Mankato, Minnesota 56003
www.capstonepub.com

Text © 2020 Fran Manushkin
Illustrations © 2020 Picture Window Books

Library of Congress Cataloging-in-Publication Data
Names: Manushkin, Fran, author. | Zarrin, Laura, illustrator.
Title: Helping Mayor Patty / by Fran Manushkin; illustrated by Laura
Zarrin.
Description: North Mankato, Minnesota : Picture Window Books, [2019]
    Series: Katie Woo's neighborhood | Summary: Katie's Aunt Patty is
    the new mayor, and Katie and her friends attend her first city council
    meeting, brimming with ideas about what their neighborhood needs—
    like free ice cream, puppies, and a new park where children can play
    in safety.
Identifiers: LCCN 2018059972| ISBN 9781515844570 (hardcover) |
    ISBN 9781515845560 (pbk.) | ISBN 9781515844617 (ebook pdf)
Subjects: LCSH: Woo, Katie (Fictitious character)—Juvenile fiction. |
    Chinese Americans—Juvenile fiction. | Mayors—Juvenile fiction. |
    Aunts—Juvenile fiction. | City councils—Juvenile fiction. | CYAC:
    Neighborhoods—Fiction. | Mayors—Fiction. | Aunts—Fiction. |
    Chinese Americans—Fiction.
Classification: LCC PZ7.M3195 Hh 2019 | DDC 813.54 [E] —dc23
LC record available at https://lccn.loc.gov/2018059972

Graphic Designer: Bobbie Nuytten

Printed and bound in the USA.
PA71

Table of Contents

BARBER

FIRE
STATION

Hospital

BAKERY

DINER

Veterinarian

Dentist

Katie's
House

N

W   E

S

Chapter 1
New Neighbors

Katie told Pedro and JoJo,
"We have a new neighbor!"

They ran to meet her.

"Hi!" said the girl. "My
name is Haley O'Hara."

"Cool name," said Katie.

"I have five brothers and sisters," Haley bragged.

"We have enough players for a soccer team," said Katie.

"Let's do it!" yelled Haley. "My brothers and sisters are already playing."

Katie's mom told her,

"You can play later. Today

is Aunt Patty's first town

meeting as our new mayor.

Let's go wish her luck."

Chapter 2
The Town Meeting

At City Hall, Mayor Patty said, "Today our city council will decide how to spend our tax money."

Katie smiled. "I love money."

"First let's begin by talking about what each neighborhood needs the most," said Aunt Patty. "Then the council will vote."

"My neighborhood is growing," said Mr. Mann. "We need a fire station."

Pedro told Katie, "Our neighborhood needs ice cream."

"Our streetlights are not bright," said Ms. Miller. "We need better ones."

"My streetlight is fine," Katie told JoJo. "I can sit by my window and read."

"I wonder what our neighborhood needs," Katie said to her friends. "I will draw a picture of our block. It will help me think."

Mr. Davis raised his

hand and said, "Please

send someone to stop pesky

squirrels from eating all my

bird food."

Mayor Patty told

Mr. Davis, "I'm sorry.

Our town can't fix that."

"I'll help you," said

Pedro's mom. "I'll show you

a better bird feeder."

An angry
man said,
"We need
more garbage
cans. Our blocks
are stinky."

"Pew!" Katie
laughed. "I'm
glad our block
is not stinky."

Katie told JoJo, "Look at my picture. What is missing from our block?"

"How about puppies in every yard?" said JoJo.

"Puppies would be fun!" said Katie. "But not necessary."

"On hot days," said Pedro, "ice cream is necessary."

"Let's think," said JoJo.
"What did we see on our
way here?"

"I saw kids playing in the
street," said Pedro. "A lot of
them!"

"That's it!" said Katie.

"Playing in the street is

dangerous. I know what our

neighborhood needs: a park!"

"A park for baseball!"

said JoJo.

"And soccer!" said Pedro.

"And sledding!" shouted

Katie.

Chapter 3
What We Need!

Katie raised her hand.

"In our neighborhood, kids

are playing in the street.

We need a park."

"Let's vote on it!" said

Mayor Patty.

The council began to
vote. They voted to spend
money on a new fire station,
better lights, more garbage
cans, and . . . a park!

On the way home,

Katie told Haley O'Hara,

"Soon there will be a big

surprise for you! Your

brothers and sisters will

like it too."

They did!

Glossary

city council (SIT-ee KOUN-suhl)—a group of people who are elected to make decisions for a city

mayor (MAY-ur)—the leader of a city government

neighborhood (NAY-bur-hud)—a smaller area within a city or town where people live and work

tax money (TAKS MUHN-ee)—money that people and businesses must pay to help support a government

vote (VOHT)—to make a choice

Katie's Questions

1. What traits make a good mayor? Would you like to be a mayor? Why or why not?

2. In cities, being a mayor is usually a full-time job. In smaller communities, the mayor often has another job too. Who is the mayor in your town or city? Does he or she have another job?

3. Now that you know who your mayor is, write him or her a letter! Share an idea you have for the city, or write and ask him or her to visit your school. An adult can help you mail your letter.

4. Imagine Aunt Patty hasn't been elected mayor yet. Make a poster asking people to vote for her. Be sure to include a reason why she would make a good mayor.

5. Compare Pedro's idea for ice cream to Katie's idea for a park. What do you think would have happened if Pedro would have asked Mayor Patty to vote for ice cream?

Dear Ms. Mayor,
Thank you for new park. It is green. I like to soccer with my friends. My dog like it too.

Ms. Mayor
ty Hall

Katie Interviews Mayor Patty!

Katie: Hello, Mayor Aunt Patty! Thanks for talking to me about your job!
Mayor Patty: Of course, Katie. It's my pleasure.

Katie: So how did you become mayor? Did you go to a special mayor class?
Mayor Patty: There's no special training to become a mayor. But you do need to win an election.

Katie: What's an election?
Mayor Patty: An election is like a contest where the winner is decided by voting. You might have voted for a class president, for example. An election for mayor works sort of the same way.

Katie: Cool! Pedro is our class president. So could anyone run for mayor? Could I run for mayor?
Mayor Patty: Someday you could! In some cities, you need to be 18 or older. Other places you have to be at least 21. And you need to live in the city where you want to serve.

Katie: What do you mean "serve"? Do you have to bring people stuff?

Mayor Patty: When I say I serve the city, I mean I offer the city my leadership. I want to help make our city a wonderful place to live. It's my job to listen and learn as much as I can. That way I can make the best decisions to help the people who live here.

Katie: Wow! Your job is really important. I'm really proud of you, Aunt Patty.

Mayor Patty: Thank you, Katie. And I tell you what . . . when you suggested that your neighbors needed a park, I was proud of you too. Keep thinking of others in your neighborhood and you'll keep making it a great place to live!

About the Author

Fran Manushkin is the author of Katie Woo, the highly acclaimed, fan-favorite early reader series, as well as the popular Pedro series. Her other books include *Happy in Our Skin, Baby, Come Out!* and the best-selling board books *Big Girl Panties* and *Big Boy Underpants*. There is a real Katie Woo: Fran's great-niece, who doesn't get into trouble like the Katie in the books. Fran lives in New York City, three blocks from Central Park, where she can often be found bird-watching and daydreaming. She writes at her dining room table, without the help of her two naughty cats, Chaim and Goldy.

About the Illustrator

Laura Zarrin spent her early childhood in the St. Louis, Missouri, area. There she explored creeks, woods, and attic closets, climbed trees, and dug for artifacts in the backyard, all in preparation for her future career as an archeologist. She never became one, however, because she realized she's much happier drawing in the comfort of her own home while watching TV. When she was twelve, her family moved to the Silicon Valley in California, where she still resides with her very logical husband and teen sons, and their illogical dog, Cody.